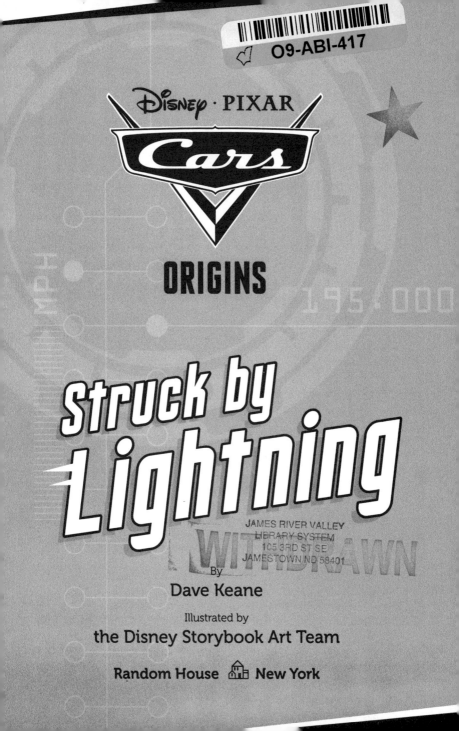

DISNEP · PIXAR

Cars

ORIGINS

Struck by Lightning

By

Dave Keane

Illustrated by

the Disney Storybook Art Team

Random House 🏠 New York

Published in the United States by Random House Children's Books, a division of Penguin Random House LLC, 1745 Broadway, New York, NY 10019, and in Canada by Penguin Random House Canada Limited, Toronto, in conjunction with Disney Enterprises, Inc. Random House and the colophon are registered trademarks of Penguin Random House LLC.

randomhousekids.com
ISBN 978-0-7364-3820-9 (trade) — ISBN 978-0-7364-8256-1 (lib. bdg.)
Printed in the United States of America
10 9 8 7 6 5 4 3 2 1

Chapter 1

"I am speed. I put the 'ace' in 'pace'. I am too fast for the fast lane."

"Uh, what are you saying there, boss?" Mack asked, rolling up alongside his soon-to-be passenger.

Lightning McQueen smiled, his eyes closed. "I am a finely tuned instrument of speed, Mack. I am gassed up, revved up, and fired up. Let's do this!"

"Whoa! You may want to take it easy, there," Mack said. "We haven't even left Radiator Springs yet. We've got three days of driving before we get to the speedway."

"I know, I know," Lightning said, opening his eyes. It's just that I've been training extra hard for this race, and now I'm ready!"

Mack chuckled. "Well, be careful you don't burn out before we even leave town."

"Don't worry, Mack. I have enough energy to race a few hundred laps right now!"

"Look at you two," Sally called from down the street. She was heading their way to wish them

both luck. "All washed, buffed, and sparkling."

"You've got to look the part, Sal," Lightning said, revving his engine.

"Sounds like he's ready to rumble," Sally said to Mack.

"He already has his sights set on the checkered flag," Mack said.

Sally laughed. "He always does. Just make sure you pace yourself, there, Stickers."

"Oh, Sal," Lightning said, smiling at her nickname for him. "You know I always do."

"You're leavin' already?" Mater said, pulling to a stop next to Lightning. "Darn it, these things just sneak up on me. I meant to do something, like make a big sign, organize a parade, or sing a song."

"Thanks, buddy. Wishing me good luck is all you need to do," Lightning replied. "No need to put yourself out."

"Oh, good, 'cause I don't really like singin' in public," Mater whispered.

"It's always too quiet around here for Mater when you're gone," Sally said.

"We all feel a little out of sorts when you leave town," said Mater.

Lightning smiled at his friends. "I wish you could all go, but this one's an extra-long haul, and just getting there will be a grind."

Luigi and Guido zoomed to a stop in front of Lightning.

"We are bringing the whitewalls," Luigi said. "Yes, yes . . . you only want the Lightyears, but Luigi never is unprepared. We bring the Fettuccine Alfredos." He motioned to Guido, who was balancing a tower of Lightyear Radials and Luigi's signature whitewalls.

"Okay, Luigi, whatever you say," Lightning said. "Guido, go ahead and load up those tires. We'll be heading out in a few minutes."

"Scusi! Scusi!" Guido said as he made his way toward Mack's trailer.

"Hey, buddy," Mater said, "maybe you can say howdy to all of us back home when you're interviewed in the winner's circle."

"Well, those TV reporters don't always have time for personal messages," Lightning said.

"Okay—then how about a secret signal?" Mater asked.

"Like what kind of signal?" Lightning asked.

"Maybe you could cross your eyes like so," Mater said, and he demonstrated. "Or roll your tongue up like this." Mater showed him. "That way we'd know you was thinkin' of us."

"Okay, Mater—I'll come up with something," Lightning said, laughing. He looked around at the cars who had gathered to see him off. "You guys are the best. But relax, everyone. I'll be back in less than a week. And when I return—"

He was interrupted by an electronic chirping coming from Mack's trailer. The phone was ringing. Lightning rolled up to the display screen and read the name.

"It's my agent," Lightning announced. "He's probably calling to tell me to get on the road."

The speaker on the phone clicked, and now everyone could hear the call.

"Hey, Harv, what's up?" said Lightning.

"Hey, Lightning. Listen, there's no good way to put this, so I'll just cut to the chase: I've got

good news and bad news for you. Which do you want first?"

"Oh," Lightning said, scrunching up his mouth as he considered his options. "Give me the good news first."

Harv paused. "The good news is there isn't going to be a race on Saturday."

"WHAT! NO!" Lightning cried. "C'mon! Seriously? But, Harv—then what's the bad news?"

Harv cleared his throat. "Uh . . . the bad news is there is no good news."

"NO RACE?" Lightning wailed. "C'mon, say it ain't so, Harv! I'm all revved up and ready to roll!"

"Hey, don't shoot the messenger." Harv's voice crackled over the speaker. "A big category two storm is heading right toward the area of the speedway. The organizers just called. The race has been delayed by at least a week, but it might be cancelled altogether."

All eyes were on Lightning now. He drooped, visibly disappointed.

"Maybe the storm will change direction," Lightning said. "Mack's trailer is all packed. I'm tuned up and ready to rumble. Let's head out anyway. We can always turn back if things don't change."

Harv hesitated and blew out a breath. "Uh, no. It already started raining there, Lightning. I checked. Sorry, but it's true what they say: You can't fight Mother Nature."

"This is a drag," Lightning said, sagging even lower.

Luigi sighed. "What bad luck! Guido had hoped to break a record for pit stops." He turned to his forklift friend. "Guido, unload the tires. We stay home."

"Okay!" said Guido.

"Hey, that reminds me," said Harv on the phone. "Luigi, I have some friends visiting from Italy. They're driving by Radiator Springs later today, and I told them to stop by your shop for a set of new tires."

"Oh, *grazie!* They will get first-class treatment at Casa Della Tires!" said Luigi. "Your friends, what do they look like?"

"They're Ferraris," Harv said.

"Did you say . . . Ferrari? In Radiator Springs? Coming to Casa Della Tires? TODAY? Quick, Guido, we must prepare!" And with that, Luigi and Guido sped off.

"Well, I guess we're staying home," said Lightning.

Sarge suddenly arrived with Fillmore. "No point in crying over spilled oil. A few of us are going camping for a couple of days. Why don't you join us?"

"Yeah, man," Fillmore said, rolling up next to Sarge. "Nothing like getting back to nature to recharge your batteries."

"Gosh, I don't know, guys," Lightning said. "I never thought of myself as a camping kind of car."

"C'mon, buddy," Mater said. "This is your chance to become a part of our annual camping trip."

"Annual?" Lightning asked. "Why haven't I ever heard of this annual camping trip before?"

"Oh," Mater said bashfully, "I guess this would be the first annual."

"I don't know...," Lightning said again, starting to back away.

Harv jumped into the conversation. "As your agent, I advise you to go. We won't know for a week if the race can be rescheduled. I think you could use some R and R."

"What does *that* mean?" Lightning grumbled.

"That stands for 'rest and relaxation,'" said Sarge. "Nothing sounds better to a soldier than a little R and R."

"I always thought 'R and R' stood for 'radiators and rims,' said Mater.

Mack smiled. "Whatever you think is best, Lightning," he said. "I wouldn't mind hanging out with my pals at the truck stop for a few days."

"The thought of you camping is something I simply can't picture." Sally giggled. "A finely tuned instrument of speed cooling his jets in the great outdoors. . . . I think it's just what you need."

"Okay, okay, you talked me into it. I'll go," Lightning said. "Waiting around here for a whole week for news will drive me crazy anyway."

"Nature, here we come!" Mater hooted, beeping his horn. "We're goin' camping!"

Chapter 2

Sarge, Fillmore, and Lightning met up at Radiator Springs city limits to head off on their big adventure. They were waiting for Mater.

"Wow, Sarge, you sure know how to prepare for a trip," Lightning said, marveling at the tightly packed trailer Sarge was pulling behind him. It contained all kinds of camping gear: tents, ropes, pots, and even firewood.

"There's no telling what we'll need, so I've brought a full battle rattle," Sarge said. "Not my first time outside the wire."

"I'm not sure what that means," Lightning said.

"Just feel the energy," Fillmore said. "Open

yourself up to some quality time with Mother Earth. The trees. The rocks. The fresh air. Can you feel the life energy flowing through you?"

"Uh, no," Lightning mumbled. "I thought we would have left by now, Sarge."

"Mater has not yet reported," Sarge said, looking back at the town. "Wait. Check that. Here he comes."

They all watched as Mater zoomed up and screeched to a stop in front of them. He was breathing hard.

"Howdy, campers!" he exclaimed.

"You're late, Mater," Sarge said.

"Oh, well, I had to say goodbye," Mater said.

"I thought you already said your goodbyes," Fillmore said.

Mater smiled. "I couldn't recall exactly who I said goodbye to, so I just said goodbye to everybody in Radiator Springs all over again. I sure do hate goodbyes."

"Really? Seems like you can't get enough of them," Fillmore said.

"All right, campers, let's move out," Sarge

said. "Remember, let's maintain the integrity of the caravan."

"Maintain the intensity of a care van?" Mater asked. "What's that mean?"

Lightning was so excited that they were finally leaving, he wasn't listening. "I'll scout ahead!" he exclaimed, and fired off like he had been shot out of a cannon. In seconds, he was no more than a red blip on the horizon.

"Would ya look at him go," said Mater. "He's faster than a yellow light in front of a police station."

"I was suggesting that we all stick together," Sarge said to Mater. "Maintain an orderly formation."

"Too late for that now," Fillmore said.

"Fall out!" Sarge barked, rolling off after Lightning.

Fillmore and Mater fell in behind Sarge.

An hour went by before they saw Lightning again. The red race car came roaring back toward them on the other side of the interstate. He exited, turned around, catapulted down the on-ramp,

then roared up alongside his three friends.

"Where have you been, buddy?" Mater asked.
"Did you already go camping?"

"Oh, sorry, guys," replied Lightning. "I've just got
lots of pent-up energy. But I can at least confirm

that the coast is clear."

Sarge couldn't help chuckling. "I guess I should expect as much, traveling with a professional race car."

Seeing that his friends weren't upset, Lightning shot ahead again. "C'mon, slowpokes!"

"He's going to get a speeding ticket," Fillmore said.

In minutes, they found Lightning waiting for them in front of a roadside shop. They saw a sign pointing toward the campgrounds.

"Wow," Fillmore said, taking in the wildflowers, dried herbs, and folk art displayed at the front of the store. "Let's not forget to stop and smell the roses."

The others waited while Fillmore browsed. Eventually, he emerged from the shop with something called a dream-catcher, which now hung from his side mirror.

"It makes you look . . . younger," said Mater. "And it's, uh . . . very slimming."

Soon they rolled off the pavement and onto a bumpy dirt road that led through the woods.

Within seconds, it became obvious that Lightning's tight suspension and low-to-the-ground frame were not ideal for the uneven terrain.

But Mater was having no problem with the rocks and bumps. "Ha! Who's the slowpoke now?" Mater hooted, driving circles around his jittery friend, kicking up dust.

Lightning coughed. "This is ridiculous! I just changed my air filter!"

"You're not worried about a few bumps and a

little dust, are you?" Sarge called back.

Lightning winced and groaned over each rock and rut in the road. "A few bumps, Sarge? I just bit my tongue back there!" He was clearly out of his element.

Fillmore pulled up alongside him. "You've gotta slow your roll a bit. We're in no hurry. Camping is all about chilling out. You can't rush relaxation. You need to ease into it."

"Oh, right," Lightning said. "It's just that . . . I'm no all-terrain vehicle."

"We all have our strengths," Fillmore said. "And weaknesses."

"Fellas, I have a special treat for y'all," Mater called. He pulled off the road and posed in front of a small wooden sign that read PINECONE FLATS. "Have you ever rolled over pinecones? It's the most satisfying crunch ever, and it just feels so darn good."

They looked out over the grassy field, which they could see was littered with large pinecones that had fallen from the surrounding trees towering over them.

"I don't know, Mater," Lightning said. "Doesn't seem like the kind of thing you should do with specialized racing tires. I don't want to get a flat."

"A flat? HA!" Mater exclaimed. "Yer not afraid of some little pinecones, are ya?"

"Don't be ridiculous," replied Lightning. "I'm just saying that it's better to be safe than sorry."

Fillmore rolled up and gazed at a pinecone. "I think it sounds groovy. Kind of like a natural remedy for stress."

"This was not part of our plan," Sarge said. "The diversion is not in line with our mission's objective for the day. And what if someone pops a tire, like Lightning suggested?"

Mater rolled his eyes and laughed. "Well, you scaredy-cars can just feast your eyes on what you're missing."

Mater cruised onto the field, and soon the pinecones were exploding under his tires with a puff of dust and a satisfying CRUNCH!

As Mater increased his speed, the sound of crunching pinecones nearly drowned out his cries of delight. "Whoooo-wheeeee!"

CRUNCH! CRUNCH! CRUNCH! CRUNCH!

"That just looks too good," Fillmore said, his eyes wide with excitement. "Time to embrace the unknown." He rolled onto the field and began driving in big, crunchy circles.

Lightning glanced at Sarge and grinned. "Well," he said, "what's the worst that can happen, right?"

And with a roar of his engine, Lightning McQueen was soon driving figure eights through the grass, pinecones exploding under his tires with amazing popping noises that echoed off the wall of trees.

"Sarge, c'mon!" the three wailed at their reluctant friend when they passed him.

"If you can't beat 'em, join 'em," Sarge finally said.

He tentatively rolled out onto the field. He stopped at the first crunch and shot his eyes around, as if he expected something bad to happen. But within seconds, he and his trailer were making big circles in the field. The thunderous *CRUNCH! CRUNCH! CRUNCH!*

sounds filled the air like a pinecone symphony.

For ten whole minutes, the foursome spun around the field and managed to locate every single dried-up pinecone. Once they had determined there were none left, they made their way back to the road, laughing and panting from the exertion.

"Whew," Mater said. "How's that for relaxing?"

Fillmore wore a silly smile. "I haven't laughed that hard since I passed my last smog test."

"I've got to admit—that was almost as good as a three-second pit stop," said Lightning.

"I've never felt such a satisfying pop," Sarge said, and his travel buddies hooted in victory at having finally won over the reluctant pinecone-crusher.

"Dadgum!" Mater shouted. "Well, in that case, let's go find some more pinecones. WHOOOOOOOOO—"

"Negative!" Sarge said, cutting him off. "It's time to get back on course."

The happy friends headed off to the campgrounds.

As evening approached, they found their campsite. It was breathtaking. Soft grass, moss-covered trees, and the trickling sound of a nearby creek—it was everything a camper could ask for.

"Wow!" Lightning exclaimed, taking in the surroundings. "You guys were right. This is amazing. I almost forgot my race was cancelled."

"No time to start hugging trees," Sarge said. "Time to pitch the tents, check the perimeter, and work out a schedule for who will stand watch tonight."

"Stand watch for what?" Lightning asked, glancing around nervously.

"Roger that, Sarge," Mater said. "Let's launch a counteroffensive, sneak up on their flanks, cut off their supply lines, then retreat for no good reason."

"What are you talking about?" Sarge said, staring at Mater.

"Oh, I have no idea," Mater said. "I just like speaking Army."

Chapter 3

The four cars were circled around a roaring fire that Sarge had started. The firewood from his trailer now crackled and popped in the otherwise quiet night. Tall orange flames jumped and danced into the star-filled sky.

Lightning looked around, waiting for someone to say or do something. After a few minutes, he broke the silence. "So, what's on tonight's agenda, guys?"

"What do you mean?" Sarge asked.

"Well, now that we got the tents up and the fire started, what are we going to do?" asked Lightning.

"This is camping," Fillmore said. "It's more

about what you're *not* doing than what you *are* doing, dig it?"

"Huh?" Lightning said. He looked at each of his friends, who seemed perfectly content in the glow of the campfire. "I mean, this is my first time camping, so . . . what happens next?"

"Nothing happens," Mater said. "That's why we love camping."

Lightning frowned. "Are you telling me we just wait around like this, then go home?"

"Oh, I almost forgot," Fillmore said. "I've got a new organic fuel recipe for us to try." He backed up into his tent, which looked different from the others. It had a dome top and was covered with painted flowers. There were also strings of colorful beads that hung down over the opening.

Fillmore returned with four small metal gas cans. "Drink up, fellas."

Once they had each received a can, they all looked at each other and sipped in silence.

"This tastes a little bit like swamp gas," Mater said, making a face.

"You guessed the secret ingredient," Fillmore said.

Lightning sighed. "Don't get me wrong—I like trying a new fuel mix as much as the next car, but I thought, you know, that more would... happen."

"You need to let yourself unwind," said Sarge. "There's more to life than racing in the fast lane all the time."

"Yeah, just chill out, man, and embrace the peaceful spirit of the forest," Fillmore said.

"Spirit? What spirit?" Lightning asked. His eyes

darted from one tree to the next.

"Oh, hey, that reminds me," Mater said. "When cars go camping, they tell ghost stories."

"I don't know any ghost stories," Sarge said. "Anybody else?"

"I used to know three good ghost stories," Fillmore said. "But I forgot two of them, and all I remember about the third one is it ended with me getting a boot on my tire and spending three days in the county impound lot."

"Shoot, that sounds like a good one," Mater said. "Hey, did I ever tell you about the Ghost Light?"

Sarge grumbled. "Oh no, not the Ghost Light story again."

"Even I remember that one," Fillmore said.

"What about the Screaming Banshee?" asked Mater.

"Heard it," the other three said at the same time.

It soon became clear that nobody knew any new ghost stories, and they fell back into silence.

"I guess it doesn't have to have a ghost in it,"

Mater said. "I could tell you the story of how I lost my left headlight."

"Go for it, buddy," said Lightning.

"It happened in one of the worst hailstorms to ever hit Carburetor County," Mater said. "I could see the black clouds approaching as the day was ending. This storm was so big and dark that it would have scared a normal storm into a sunny day. I was racing back from a tow. I had just helped a mail truck who had gotten himself stuck in a ditch. He was panicking because of the approachin' storm."

"I thought those guys delivered the mail no matter what," Sarge said. "They're always bragging that 'rain or shine, snow or sleet, we deliver your mail.'"

"But notice that their motto doesn't mention hail," Fillmore said. "It does mention sleet, but not hail."

"Wait a second—isn't sleet the same thing as hail?" Lightning asked. "Sleet is just frozen rain, like hail, right?"

"Okay, let's not turn Mater's headlight story

into a weather forecast," Sarge said.

Mater drew up close to the fire. His eyes grew wide with fear. "Yeah, this was one of the most scariest moments of my life!"

"Go ahead, Mater," Fillmore said, "before I forget how this story started."

"So there I was, driving back to Radiator Springs, trying to beat the storm 'fore it arrived, but I don't make it."

"What do you mean, you don't make it?" Lightning asked.

Mater winced and his whole body shook at the memory. "The hail was harmless at first, like tiny grains of sand. Then it was as big as pebbles. It started to hurt. Soon they was as big as ball bearings. Then lug nuts! The faster I went, the more dents I got. I was as nervous as a balloon at a cactus farm."

The others stared, imagining the terrible scene in their minds.

Mater continued, and he began to shake from bumper to bumper. "Suddenly, the hail was as big as rocks. It was like a thousand hammers beating down on me. And there weren't no place to hide! I was out in the open country, going full speed in the dark. I closed one eye as them hailstones became as big as boulders."

"Boulders?" Lightning, Sarge, and Fillmore said at the same time.

Mater's mouth dropped open as he recalled the scene. Then he swallowed hard, and another tremor moved through his body.

"I figured I was heading to my final parking spot," Mater said. "And just when I thought it couldn't get no worse, those icy hail balls became bigger than me, and they was crashing down with thunderous booms, shaking the ground beneath me like it was a blanket. I flew so high in the air, I could see all the way to Crankshaft County!"

"Hold it right there, Mater," said Sarge. "Hail doesn't get that big. You're putting us on!"

Mater squinted at Sarge. "One doesn't forget a single detail of a near-death experience."

"Ha, ha, ha," said Lightning. "Next you're going to tell us that a UFO came crashing down to Earth!"

"That's a whole 'nother story," said Mater. "This time, it was just really big hail. It was like raining glaciers!"

"Mater, that's impossible," said Lightning.

"Well, where do ya think Carburetor Canyon came from? A huge hailstone dropped down and done created that canyon," said Mater.

"What?" exclaimed Lightning.

"Anyhoo, them vibrations from the hail hitting the ground were so intense, they shook a headlight right out of me."

"Wait—I don't get it," Lightning said, looking at Sarge and Fillmore. "Is this true? How can this be true?"

Mater turned to Lightning with wide eyes. "My headlight is still out there in the desert somewhere. Who knows if it'll ever get found. I'm just countin' my blessings I had the good sense to hold the other one in place with my tow hook. Otherwise, I'd be standing in front of you tonight with neither headlight."

After several seconds of silence, all four of them burst into laughter.

When the laugher died down, Lightning looked confused. "I still don't get it. Was any part of that story true?"

Sarge chuckled. "Mater, that was an outstanding performance. The tall tale is a campfire storytelling tradition."

"Tall tale? Who said anything about a tall tale?" asked Mater.

The other campers paused and looked at one another, bewildered.

"There's no way—" Sarge began.

Just then, a flash of lightning lit up the sky to the west, followed seconds later by a low rumble of thunder.

"Watch, it'll probably hail now," Fillmore said.

"I like lightning!" exclaimed Mater as he gazed up into the sky. "It's purty."

"Aw, thanks, Mater," said Lightning. "I think you're pretty, too."

The campers burst into another round of laughter.

"You know, Lightning," said Sarge, "I've always wondered how you got your name. I never knew anyone named Lightning before I met you."

Lightning looked at his friends. "It's a name that sort of just happened."

"You mean you just woke up one day and you had a different name? Far out," said Fillmore.

"Well, kind of, I guess. I just got that name one day and it stuck," replied Lightning.

Mater looked stunned. "You mean Lightning wasn't always yer name?" he asked.

"Nope," said Lightning. "My original name

was . . . uh . . . something else."

"What was it?" asked Fillmore.

"It was, um . . ." Lightning's voice trailed off as he mumbled something.

"Say again? We couldn't hear that," said Sarge.

"Monty," Lightning finally said. "My original name was Monty McQueen."

Mater's, Fillmore's, and Sarge's mouths fell open. Then they all exclaimed at once: "MONTY?"

"Are you putting us on?" Fillmore said. "Monty McQueen? With a name like that, you could have hosted your own daytime game show!"

"My uncle's name was Monty. He was the slowest car I ever knew," said Sarge. "Lightning suits you much better."

"Thanks, Sarge. I always thought so," Lightning said. "Hey, would you guys like to hear how I got my new name?"

"Oh, goody," Mater said. "I can't wait to tell everybody back in Radiator Springs."

"Hey, this story is only for you guys," Lightning said.

"Yeah, what happens at the campsite stays at

the campsite," Fillmore said.

"They call it the circle of campfire trust," said Sarge.

"Oh, I get it," Mater said. "This is like a secret society! Huh? What society? I have no idea what you're talking about! See—yer secret is safe with me."

"Okay," Lightning said, taking a deep breath. "I don't know any ghost stories, tall tales, or funny stories, but I do know my own story. So let me tell you how I became Lightning McQueen."

Chapter 4

"Nobody knew me at the Fast Track Race Academy when I arrived. Nobody had ever heard the name Lightning McQueen, because I was still Monty McQueen at that time. I didn't really stand out in any way. I was like every other student at the academy—a wide-eyed racer who could only hope of getting a pro circuit sponsorship one day. Making it all the way to the Piston Cup seemed like a pipe dream. But I knew a race of a thousand miles began by crossing the starting line. All I needed was a chance to show what I could do.

Within days of my arrival, I teamed up with the academy's top racer, a young stock car named Carl. We hit it off immediately. We did everything together. Raced. Studied. Shared strategies. Dreamed of fame and fortune.

Only the top five racers in the final race of the school semester got a sponsorship deal, so Carl and I planned and plotted on how we'd get two of those spots. There was some impressive talent at the academy, but we knew we were the best race cars there.

Every morning, just as the sun was coming up, we'd hit the school track and run laps all by ourselves. We practiced holding our turns, got as close to the wall as we dared, and even raced against each other. Carl loved the sport just as much as I did. That's why we were such an awesome team.

The final race of the semester was quickly approaching, and everyone was vying for one of those five spots. Carl was as determined to win as I was. And we had put in the work. We were ready. But the night before the race, I was so excited, I couldn't sleep. When I finally dozed off, I overslept. I woke up late! I was feeling frazzled

and out of sorts when I arrived just minutes before the race was about to begin.

'Monty!' Carl called. 'Where have you been?'

'I overslept a bit, but I've never been more ready for anything,' I told him.

'Whoa, your rear left wheel looks loose,' he said. 'Let's get those lug nuts tightened.'

He sent one of his pitties over, and before I

knew it, I was all fixed up.

'Thank goodness I noticed, Monty,' Carl said. 'But that's what friends are for, right?'

'I can't thank you enough, Carl,' I said, rolling into my position with the forty-five other students who had qualified for the race. 'Good luck!' I called to him.

Carl winked at me from three rows back.

I closed my eyes for a brief second. This was it. This was my chance to shine. When the green flag dropped, I roared louder than all the

other racers, but something was wrong.

My rear left wheel flew off before I had even reached the starting line.

'NOOOOOOO!' I screamed.

I couldn't believe it. My mind spun in confusion. I watched my wheel roll and bounce away into the infield. I could hear the gasps from the crowd in the stands.

'Sorry, pal!' Carl shouted as he passed me. 'It's every car for himself today. And I needed to put the odds in my favor!'

I was shocked. He had asked his pitty to *remove* the lug nuts—not tighten them!

'I thought you were my friend!' I cried, but he was already long gone.

I limped off the track. I was devastated, embarrassed, and furious. 'You can't count on anyone,' I said to myself when I returned to the garage.

Carl got a sponsorship deal that day and left the academy. I never saw him again. Carl's dream came true and I was left with nothing. I had always planned to leave the academy early and head straight to the pros. But all that had changed.

I returned to the academy after a two-week break, and I was determined to work alone. I preferred to spend time by myself. I avoided my classmates, studied late into the night, and I promised myself to never trust anyone again. I still woke up before dawn and got in a hundred laps before any other car was awake. I pushed myself harder than I ever had with Carl, because now I had something to prove.

The academy's monthly twenty-five-lap sprint was my next chance to show what I could do. All the hurt and frustration poured out of me in that race. I shocked everyone by breaking the academy's all-time record.

I earned the nickname Lightning from my fellow racers that very day. And the name stuck. Nobody ever called me Monty again.

All the attention was great. I loved the respect and admiration. But when everyone suddenly wanted to be my friend, I backed away. After my experience with Carl, I wasn't going to get chummy or team up with anyone. I truly believed I could make it to the pro circuit one day, but I also believed I could only count on myself. I was set on being a one-car race team.

Now that I look back on everything, I have to say I'm kind of grateful for Carl. If it weren't for that wheel coming off at the start of that race so many years ago, I might still be known as Monty. And I probably wouldn't have wound up in Radiator Springs to meet some of the greatest friends a car could ever ask for."

Chapter 5

Mater had been hanging on every word of Lightning's story. When Lightning finished, Mater jumped up and yelled, "Whooo-wheee!" he exclaimed. "That there's the best tall tale I've ever heard!"

"What? No, Mater, that story is one hundred percent true." said Lightning.

"Shoot, I was afraid you were gonna say that," said Mater. "Now I'm not sure what to call you anymore. To be truthful, I kinda like Monty! Monty McQueen—that has a real nice ring to it. Can I call you Monty?"

"Nobody has called me that in forever," Lightning said. "That's not my name anymore.

That'd be like calling Fillmore a name like Stan, and addressing Sarge as Corporal."

"It's Sarge," Sarge said, looking stern. "I earned each one of these stripes."

Mater had been inspired by all the racing in Lightning's story. He started to drive in circles around the campfire, going as fast as he could within the circle of light. "My favorite part was when you was racin' in the morning as the sun was just peeking up," he said. "There you was, you and that no-good Carl. The morning breeze blowin' in yer face. Battlin' it out on the track before anyone even woked up."

"Careful, Mater," Sarge said, moving back.

As soon as the words left Sarge's mouth, Mater's tow hook accidently caught on the handle of Fillmore's gas can. When Mater came to an abrupt stop, the can swung over the fire, instantly burst into a ball of flames, and ignited Mater's rear bumper.

"BE RIGHT BACK!" Mater shouted, zooming off like a meteor through the night sky.

"Whoa. What just happened?" Fillmore asked.

"Hope that water is closer than it sounds," Lightning said.

The three campers watched the glow in the trees as Mater drove through them like a torch.

Soon they heard a splashing sound and the hiss of steam, and then the light in the forest was snuffed out.

Within minutes, Mater returned, his rear end still smoking. "Whew, that was close."

"I'd say that was a bit closer than close, man," Fillmore said.

"We need to use caution and respect around this fire at all times," Sarge told the campers.

"Glad you're okay, Mater," Lightning said.

"I think I'm gladder than you. My hindquarters is almost medium rare."

Sarge turned to Lightning. "Thank you for sharing your story, Lightning. Even painful experiences can make us better. Your story reminded me of a time I was stationed overseas and was late for my transport ship."

"What? I never knew you were late for anything," Fillmore said.

Sarge blew out a breath of air. "Well, it wasn't my fault. There was a sergeant in another unit who didn't like me. He had conspired to get me off that ship."

"Wow, that sounds serious, Sarge," said Lightning.

"It was embarrassing, that's what it was," said Sarge. "It all happened during a weekend furlough, which is like a free pass in the army to go have some fun. And that's what I did. I was young and foolish."

"Party on, Sarge," Fillmore said. "Who knew you ever had fun."

Sarge gave Fillmore a sideways glance. "I was on my way back to my ship after a night on the town when I ran across a cute little sports car who had run out of gas. I stopped to help her, as any gentlecar would, but we soon got to talking, and then she wanted to head back into town for a pint of oil. I completely lost track of time. Before I knew it, it was midnight!"

"And you made the whole ship wait for you to show up?" Mater asked.

"Oh, no," Sarge said with a sigh. "They left without me. Took me a few weeks to catch up with them. It was humiliating. I spent countless nights mopping every deck on that ship."

"You should have know'd better," Mater said with a chuckle. "We do crazy things for love."

"It wasn't love, Mater. It was a setup! That other sergeant had asked the little sports car to delay me so I'd miss the ship," said Sarge.

"Ooooh! That other sarge is just as bad as Carl!" exclaimed Mater. "What did you do?"

"I couldn't do much, except learn from my mistake," said Sarge.

The four shared a quiet moment. A chorus of crickets filled in the spaces between the crackles and pops from the fire.

"Okay, Mater," Fillmore said. "How about one more story before we turn in for the night?"

"Aw, shucks," Mater said. "I think we'd all rather hear about what happened to Monty after he became Lightning."

"Agreed," Sarge said. "So, Lightning, how did you go from the academy to the Piston Cup?"

"Yeah, man, were you an instant rock star?" Fillmore asked.

"Did you start getting recognized on the street?" Sarge asked.

"Whoa! Whoa!" Lightning said. "Guys, it wasn't like that. Sure, I had gotten a cool name and was suddenly a lot more popular at school, but that was only the beginning. That 'overnight success' stuff is a myth."

"When did you get on TV?" Mater asked. "I always wanted to be on TV 'cause I'm so handsome when lit properly."

"Okay, hold on," Lightning said, laughing. "If you three settle down and stop asking me so many questions, I'll tell you the next chapter of my story."

Chapter 6

"While I wasn't an overnight success, there was no doubt I was starting to get noticed. I always had raw talent, but Carl's betrayal gave me drive.

As I entered my final months at the Fast Track Race Academy, I continued to study and excel. Every spare moment I had was dedicated to becoming a better racer. I studied films of famous Piston Cup races. I read books about the all-time greats. I even turned two checkered flags into curtains in my dorm room. As they say, I was in it to win it.

I was the big car on campus, but everywhere I went, I heard others whispering about what Carl had done to me. As if I needed to be reminded.

55

The fact that he was off racing for a sponsor and I wasn't is what got me out on that track every day.

As my time at the academy came to a close, it became clear that I was on the radar of an amateur-league racing team. They had come out on several occasions to scout me and had seen me win several school races. After I graduated at the top of my class, I was approached by the coach. He wanted to sign me to the team, but he let me know up front that I wouldn't be a sponsored racer. I might get a sponsorship one day, but I'd have to earn it.

Sure, it wasn't the offer I had hoped for and dreamed about, but it would get me into some real races. I accepted the offer.

When I joined my new race team, the other racers didn't look all that thrilled about my arrival. Coach said I'd need a number to compete.

'He looks like a 0 to me,' one of my new teammates muttered.

'Can I have number 7?' I asked Coach. 'That's my lucky number.'

'No,' Coach said.

'Okay, then how about 13?' I said. 'Everyone thinks that's an unlucky number, but I'm the type who can make his own luck.'

'No,' Coach said.

'Okay. How about 25? That's an odd number, but I'm okay with being an odd car.'

'No.'

'11? That's a prime number, and I'm a prime race car.'

'No.'

'33?'

'No.'

'How am I going to pick a number if you keep saying no to every one I throw out?'

Coach rolled his eyes. 'Because you don't get to pick your number. That's not how it works. You get assigned the number that this team has available.'

'Oh,' I said, disappointed.

The other racers laughed at my surprise.

'He doesn't have a clue,' said a hulking green racer named Wiley.

'You're going to be number 95,' Coach said, showing me the decals I'd soon be wearing.

'WHAT?' I yelped. 'But that's a terrible number! Who would want to be 95? That doesn't sound fast at all.'

'The number 95 sounds perfect to me,' Wiley said, loud enough for everybody to hear. 'Looks

like he'll always be a nickel short of a dollar.'

Another car rolled up. 'Let's hope you do better than the last car on our team who wore that number. Right now he's up in that big wrecking yard in the sky.'

'He is?' I gulped.

That got another round of chuckles from the other cars.

I didn't let it get to me. I knew they were just worried about me stealing the limelight. They had heard about my record-breaking times. Plus, nobody likes the new guy.

That's when I decided to make the most of my situation. 'All right,' I said to myself, 'if 95 is the number they're giving me, then that's the number I'll make famous one day.'

Just as I did at school, I felt like a bit of an outsider on my new team, but I worked hard and let my speed do the talking. My confidence soared as I realized those cars had nothing on me. When they zigged, I zagged. When they wouldn't let me pass, I outsmarted them. When they pressed up from behind and tried to crowd me, I left them in the dust.

At our first race, we faced off against a bigger, better-known team. My team hadn't beaten them in a long time. 'This year will be different,' I told my fellow racers. 'They've never seen anything like Lightning McQueen before.'

'That's because cars like you are usually so far behind them,' Wiley said.

Well, that day I gave every racer on the track a taste of what Lightning could do. I started out fast, opened up a sizeable lead, and gave each of them a wink as I lapped them.

There was a pair of sleek steel-gray racers on our rival team. They looked like twins, and neither liked getting shown up by the new car. They tried to squeeze me, pin me in, and slow me down so one of their teammates could catch up. When I went right, they went right. When I tried to push past on the inside, they cut me off. So I divided and conquered. After coming out of a turn, I faked toward the wall and revved my engine, and one of them shot that way. Then I quickly cut to the inside, drawing the other twin in for a block.

That left the space between them open for a split second—and that was all I needed. I threaded that needle and shot right through.

I could hear each of them blaming the other as I pulled away.

I won that first race by *two laps*, and as a result, I gained the reluctant admiration of my teammates.

'Wow, the last guy wearing that number never won a single race,' Wiley told me.

'Say hello to the new number 95,' I said.

'You're the real deal, Lightning,' a young racer named Julio told me.

'You just broke our twelve-year losing streak to that team,' Coach said. 'I think I was right about you, Lightning.'

I'm not going to lie—it felt great to win. My confidence was soaring.

An hour after that race, I got a call from a talent agent named Harv. He told me he had been at the race and said he had a sponsor all lined up—if I'd let him represent me, of course.

The sponsor was a company called Smell

Swell. Certainly not the kind of sponsor a racer dreams of landing, but it was a sponsor nonetheless. And they were in the Piston Cup. At that time, helping cars with their odor issues sounded like a pretty noble cause to me.

I was on my way. My hard work, dedication, and focus were finally paying off. I don't think I had ever been that excited in my life.

Then Harv told me my name was in the latest issue of *Racing Weekly* magazine. I had made it on a list of young racers to keep an eye on.

Without thinking, I shouted, *'Ka-chow!'* into the phone.

When Harv asked me what the heck *"ka-chow"* meant, I told him I wasn't exactly sure.

'It just came to me. Hey, I guess that's the sound that lightning makes when it strikes. Get it? Lightning strikes.'

'I get it,' Harv said. 'But lightning doesn't make any noise. That's thunder.'

'C'mon, Harv—don't spoil the fun. Let's face it: you can't fight true inspiration.'"

Chapter 7

The early-morning clouds hung dark and low, and the mist over the campground turned into a light rain. Sarge rolled out of his tent, and, just as he had done in the army, he blasted a bugle call to signal to his fellow campers that it was time to start the day.

"Are you kidding me, Sarge?" Lightning croaked as he rolled out of his tent, his eyes heavy with sleep. "It feels like we just turned in for the night."

"You just ruined a fabulous dream, Sarge," Fillmore said from inside his tent.

"At least you had a dream, Fillmore. You kept me up half the night with your snoring. You should really see someone about that," said Lightning.

"Allergies, man," Fillmore replied.

"Holy hood ornament!" Mater cried, emerging from the woods. "This rain is giving that creek ideas."

"I've never known you to be such an early riser, Mater," Lightning said, yawning.

"Not usually," Mater said, "but you was talkin' in your sleep. Something 'bout not needing to make a pit stop. Sounded pretty important."

"You should really see someone about that, Lightning," Fillmore said as he came out of his tent.

"Ugh—sorry, Mater," Lightning said. "Some cars dream about flying, I always dream about racing."

"Oh, that's okay," Mater said. "I dreamed I was being chased by a herd of angry hail balls , but it was more of a funny dream than a nightmare."

The small fire Sarge had started was hissing as it struggled against the light rain.

"Camping and rain seem like a bad combo," Lightning said.

"I'll heat up a fresh pot of oil," Fillmore said. "Who likes theirs black?"

"Who doesn't?" Lightning said.

"Count me in," Sarge said. "Nothing like a hot cup of motor oil to start the day off right."

They gathered around the small fire and waited for the oil to warm up.

"I was thinkin' about your 'ka-chow' story," said Mater, rolling up next to Lightning.

"*Ka-chow,*" Lightning said without his normal energy. It was too early.

"Just wonderin' if you ever considered somethin' else, like maybe . . . 'ka-chingle'?"

"What?" Lightning said. "Mater, that sounds ridiculous."

Fillmore joined in. "What about 'ka-chowza'?"

"'*Ka-chowza*'?" Lightning said. "That's the silliest thing I—"

"I kind of like 'ka-choo'!" said Sarge.

"Gesundheit!" Mater replied.

Lightning made a face. "This is what I get for telling you guys a very personal story."

They all shared a good laugh.

The rain began to fall harder, and the four friends eventually drove down to take a look at the rising creek. The water was much higher than they'd expected. The wooden bridge that connected their campsite to the rest of the campground was already under a foot of water.

A bolt of lightning flashed, and moments later, the sky rumbled with thunder.

"I'd feel better if we occupied the high ground," Sarge said.

By the time they got back to their campsite, their tents were flapping wildly in the wind, and the swaying trees threatened to snap.

Sarge didn't look happy. "I don't like this one bit. This wind means business, and the rain isn't letting up. There are hills about two klicks to the east of us. Just to be safe, let's go there and wait this rain out."

"How far is a klick?" Lightning asked.

Sarge smiled. "It's a kilometer, something *you* usually drive in a few seconds. This will take longer."

"No kidding," Lightning said, pulling a tire out of the thick mud.

Squinting, they made their way through the fierce rain.

"I scouted this area when we arrived, and I spotted some caves in those hills!" Sarge shouted, leading the way. "We'll be safe there."

Lightning tried to stay close to Sarge and the others, but he quickly fell behind. With the torrential rain, there was hardly any visibility.

Suddenly on his own, Lightning stopped.

"SARGE, WHERE ARE YOU?"

There was no answer.

Lightning continued to inch forward. His racing tires kept slipping and spinning in the muck. "This is crazy," he mumbled. "I'd be warm and cozy right now if Mack and I were headed to the race like we were supposed to be."

Lightning finally reached one of the caves and shook the rain off. His friends were nowhere in sight. "At least it's dry in here," he said.

He drove inside. The cave was completely dark. "Hello?" he called, his voice echoing. "Sarge? Fillmore? Mater?"

He felt his way in the darkness, then stopped short when he touched something. He was suddenly blinded by a bright light.

"AARGH!" Lightning yelled.

"Sorry," said Mater, turning so his headlight was no longer shining into Lightning's eyes. "I fell asleep. What took you so long?"

"Mater! You scared me!" Lightning exclaimed. "Where are Sarge and Fillmore?"

"Follow me!" Mater said.

Mater sped deeper into the cave, and Lightning did his best to stay on his tail so he didn't lose the light—or his friend.

"WHOOOOO-WHEEEEEE!" Mater howled in the confined space, turning left and right into connecting caves.

"Slow down!" Lightning hollered as he struggled to navigate the cave's uneven terrain.

"Where's the fun in slowing down?" Mater said.

After a sudden, steep plunge, they stopped short in a large, dark space with a fire flickering on the floor. They were relieved to see Sarge and Fillmore waiting for them in the shadows.

"Welcome to our cave party," Fillmore said.

"Come get warm, Lightning," Sarge said. "You're still dripping."

"Mater, how did you ever find this place through all those tunnels?" Lightning asked.

"Dumb luck," Mater said.

"This is perfect for telling more of your story, Lightning," Fillmore said.

"You really want to hear more?" Lightning asked, rolling up to the glow of the fire.

"All other activities for this morning have been cancelled," Sarge said.

"And we could use a good story to take our minds off our soggy tents," Fillmore said.

"And my flat," Sarge said, raising a front tire into the light. It was clearly deflated.

Mater inspected Sarge's tire. "I can help you

swap that out for your spare."

"Okay, while Sarge gets fixed up, I'll provide some distraction," Lightning said. "So—I told you how I got my nickname, my number, and my catchphrase. Why don't I tell you how everything soon went downhill from there?"

Chapter 8

"I was always under the impression that once you had an official sponsor, you had it made. I thought it would be like getting to the other side of a great big wall. The grass would be greener, the racetracks would be freshly paved, and all the fuel would be high-octane.

But I was mistaken.

Smell Swell was no Dinoco, or even Rust-eze, for that matter. Not by a long shot. Turns out most cars don't mind a little odor. Business wasn't great, so everything was on a tight budget. That included the cost of my hauler. The news really hit me hard the day before my first big race with Smell Swell as my sponsor.

See, a racer like me counts on his hauler to get him to the right race at the right time in the right condition. I trust Mack with my life. He's always reliable. But Snyder, my Smell Swell hauler, was nothing like Mack. In fact, Snyder couldn't hold Mack's mud flaps. Let's just say he was a few pistons short of a full engine block.

Snyder was a flatbed tow trailer, so I was tied down and covered with canvas when we were on the road, which was bad because Snyder needed help with directions. He got lost. A lot.

We got lost three times on the way to my first race. We eventually arrived at the Texas International Raceway—which would've been fantastic if the race was actually being held there.

'Are you kidding me, Snyder?' I wailed. 'We're supposed to be at the Arizona State National Speedway. How could you miss my race by two states?'

'We're not in Arizona? Well, that explains why all the stadium lights are off,' Snyder said.

'I can't believe this,' I said. 'The race starts tomorrow at noon. We'll never make it.'

'Well, jump back on,' he replied. 'I'll drive east all night, and if I don't get pulled over for speeding, we should get there before the race starts.'

'Drive east?' I hollered. 'Snyder, Arizona is to the west of us.'

'Really?' he said, biting his lip. 'Since when?'

When he said that, I should have just headed off to Arizona on my own. But I didn't want to abandon Snyder, so I jumped back on the flatbed and he pulled away. 'Just follow the sunset,' I told him.

'Okay! Los Angeles International Speedway, here we come!' exclaimed Snyder.

'What? NO! We're going to the Arizona State National Speedway!' I yelled.

'Yeah, that's what I meant,' he replied.

I took a deep breath and closed my eyes. It was going to be a long trip.

I eventually cooled off and fell asleep under my flapping canvas. I was having a great dream about Dinoco when I woke up in a panic. Snyder was driving like a maniac! I held on for dear life

as we careened from one side of the freeway to other. After what seemed like an eternity, we finally came to a stop.

'Huh . . . two blowouts at the same time. Talk about bum luck,' Snyder said.

'Wh-where are we?' I asked, trying to catch my breath.

'I'm not exactly sure,' he said. 'Somewhere between where we started and where we're going.'

'Why did I even ask?' I muttered. 'Okay, let's get you patched up. Where do you keep your spare tires?'

'They haven't arrived yet.'

'Arrived?'

'Well, I requested some spare tires from Smell Swell. I had to figure out these really complicated business-expense forms. I thought they'd get to me before we left, but I guess they're still on their way.'

'Wait, are you're telling me you have no spare tires with you right now?' I asked.

'I've got two,' he said.

'Oh, thank goodness! For a second there, I thought—'

'But I'm already using them. They're up here in the front. I had two flats before I picked you up, so I had to put on my spares.'

It was all I could do to keep from crying. 'I don't think you can still call it a spare tire if you're actually using it!'

So we had to wait two hours for a tire delivery, and then I had trouble sleeping, for fear that Snyder would lose his way again.

That's what it was like for every race.

We'd get lost, Snyder would get a flat, and I'd arrive frazzled and yawning.

Before long, I got the reputation as a fast starter but a weak finisher. Nobody could keep up with me at the green flag. I would smoke 'em all in the first seventy-five laps or so, but by the time they waved the checkered flag, I needed a nap.

I was so sleepy and exhausted from helping Snyder navigate, everybody started questioning my stamina. And even my desire to win.

Harv called and said my sponsor was disappointed with my performance. Can you imagine the nerve of those guys? 'They're not thrilled with your back-of-the-pack finishes,' he told me.

'Neither am I!' I shouted.

I was stuck between a rock and a Snyder. It was hopeless.

That's when a shiny red Rust-eze hauler visited me at a very slow Smell Swell publicity event. He was the only one waiting to take a photo with me.

'I used Smell Swell once,' he told me. 'But that

perfumey odor made me dizzy.'

'I don't think you're the only one,' I replied. 'Hey, thanks for stopping by.'

'My name's Mack,' he said. 'And I just wanted to pop over and say that I'm a big fan. You're one of the best racers out there.'

'With all my last-place finishes, I'm not sure I can agree with you, but thanks.'

'Don't get down on yourself, Lightning McQueen. You've got the right stuff,' Mack said, rolling off. 'I'll see you around.'

After another middle-of-the-pack finish at my next race, Mack returned with the two owners of Rust-eze: Rusty and Dusty.

'My brother and I think you've got some real potential,' Rusty said.

'Yeah, and we want to make a bet on red,' Dusty said.

'Huh?' I said.

Rusty laughed. 'What my brother is trying to say is we want you to come and race on our team.'

Dusty nodded. 'How'd you like to be the

spokescar for Rust-eze?'

'We already called your agent, Harv, and worked out the details,' Rusty said. 'If you're willing, we're ready when you are.'

'Ka-chow!' I said. 'You bet! I can't believe it!'

'You can even keep your number,' Rusty said. 'We've got the number 95 available.'

'Double ka-chow!' I said, flashing them my best Lightning McQueen smile.

'Is that your lightning sound?' Rusty asked. 'Because I don't think lightning makes a noise. That's thunder.'

'My brother, the wet blanket,' Dusty said. 'Don't mind him. You keep ka-chowing all you want.'

I was so excited, I asked if I could help design my own paint job. They said sure. So I came up with a golden lightning bolt behind the 95.

'WE LOVE IT!' Rusty and Dusty shouted when I showed it to them.

I had a good feeling that things were going to change for the better. And they did."

Chapter 9

"**W**hoa, check out the double rainbow," said Fillmore as he emerged from the cave.

The rain had finally stopped, and the sun was peeking out from the parting clouds. Waves of steam rose from the soaked earth.

"Last one back to camp is a rotten radiator!" Mater said, shooting out of the cave and flying down the hillside with reckless abandon.

"I'll take that challenge, Mater!" Lightning hollered as he sped after his friend. His engine roared as his wheels sent up streams of wet grass behind him.

"Proceed with caution!" Sarge called out.

Fillmore, who was parked in front of the cave,

looked back at Sarge and grinned. "Eat my grass, Sarge," he said, and proceeded to spin his wheels in the thick grass. "WAAAIT UUUP!" Fillmore wailed as he bounced down the hill.

Sarge stared as Fillmore whooped his way toward Lightning and Mater. "They look like clown cars at the circus," he muttered to himself. He rolled out of the cave, looking a bit uncertain about his new tire. "Well, time to throw caution to the wind," he said. And with that, he went rambling down the bumpy hillside, unable to keep himself from hollering like the others.

Little did the four know, they had exited out of a different cave from the one they'd entered. They were now slipping and sliding down the wrong side of the hill, traveling away from their campsite instead of toward it.

They traveled that way for almost twenty minutes, each bragging that he'd be the first one to reach camp. Their voices seemed to carry for miles through the dripping woods.

"Maybe we should hold up!" Sarge shouted to the others. "Nothing looks familiar!"

"Nice try, Sarge!" Fillmore yelled back. "You're just mad you're in last place!"

They all kept driving as fast as they could. Mater was in first place. Sarge had moved into second. Lightning was closing the distance in third place. His Lightyears were clearly not designed for the slick conditions.

Fillmore was huffing and puffing far behind the other three. "Maybe Sarge was right. We better stop and figure out where we are."

At that moment, the three cars in front suddenly rolled into a steep ravine. Mater was the first to bump and bounce dangerously fast down the rocky slope, soon followed by Sarge, then Lightning. They were so focused on staying on all four wheels, they didn't even have time to call out a warning to Fillmore. He drove over the edge of the ravine, too, his wheels kicking up an avalanche of small rocks and dirt.

They met at the bottom of the ravine, all looking relieved to have survived.

"Didn't see that one coming," Fillmore said.

"And I thought *racing* was dangerous," Lightning said. "A drive in the woods can get ugly fast."

"That was indeed dangerous," Sarge said.

"Somebody dug a big hole where our

campsite was," Mater said, looking around, bewildered.

"No, this can't be the right place," Lightning said. "We got lost somehow."

"Blast it—I knew we were heading the wrong way," Sarge said, disappointed in himself. "That's what I was trying to tell you back there. I should have never left camp without a compass."

"Now what?" Lightning said. "We're stuck down here!"

"It'll get dark soon," Sarge said.

"I miss my tent," said Fillmore.

The four blinked up at the steep slope of the ravine, seeing the spot where they had driven over the edge.

"I don't know about you, but this ain't nothin'," Mater said, whipping his cable hook around and then flinging it up and over the edge of the ravine. High above, the cable looped around the trunk of a tree, and the hook attached securely on the cable.

"Bye, now," Mater said, and he pulled himself backward up the side of the ravine. The others watched with shocked admiration. "You should see yer faces right now. You look like someone stole your brakes."

"Impressive," Sarge whispered.

Soon Mater reached the top of the ravine and

looked down at his companions. "Well, that was fun. I guess I'll see y'all back at the campsite!" he said, and disappeared.

"NOOOOOO!" Sarge, Fillmore, and Lightning screamed.

"Just kiddin'," Mater said, suddenly reappearing. "Who's first?" He tossed his hook down to his three stuck friends.

When they were all back up, they headed back in the direction they had come.

"Mater, that was amazing," Lightning said. "You saved us."

"It was like being evacuated by the Special Forces," Sarge said.

"Aw, shucks, I'm just doin' my job," Mater said. "I never go nowhere without my trusty tow cable. Comes in handy more than you think. I even floss with it."

"Okay, that was an overshare," Lightning said.

The drive back to the campsite was uneventful. The group had learned their lesson about racing through the woods. They took their time and made sure to stick together.

"Remember when I complained about doing nothing while we sat around the campfire?" Lightning said.

"Yep, you was bored," replied Mater.

"Well, I take it back," said Lightning. "All I want to do now is sit by that fire and do nothing."

"You're in luck, camper! We've arrived!" Sarge exclaimed.

"Campsite, sweet campsite," Mater said.

"It appears that our tents have successfully weathered the storm," Sarge said, inspecting them one by one.

Soon the four exhausted friends were gathered around a crackling fire again, and Fillmore made another batch of his organic fuel mix. The hungry campers were grateful.

"The first time I camped out was at Carstock," Fillmore said. "It was an outdoor concert at a farm. All the greatest musicians were there. And there were cars as far as you could see, all dancing in the mud and celebrating peace and togetherness. It was beautiful, man."

"That sounds like a hoot," Mater said.

"Sounds more like a bunch of hippies ruining a farmer's field." Sarge gave Fillmore a disapproving look.

"It was a little of both," admitted Fillmore. "It was the grooviest concert I've ever been to. And camping right there, in the middle of all the action, was far out. I was just bummed that I had to miss the last day. I had somehow ended up in the county impound. My memory gets a little hazy about it."

"Ever notice a lot of your stories end that way?" Sarge said.

"Do they? I don't remember," said Fillmore. "But, man, I do remember that the impound lot is totally not cool," said Fillmore. "I learned the hard way."

"I spent a night in an impound lot when I first arrived in Radiator Springs," said Lightning. "I woke up with a parking boot on my tire. Remember that, Mater?"

"Course I remember! That's when I met my best friend," Mater replied.

Mater and Lightning exchanged a smile and

bumped tires.

"Well, you don't usually make friends at the impound," said Fillmore. "You just wait there behind the fence, thinking about where you went wrong. That's tough."

"Tougher than those two weeks of intensive pit-crew training with Doc?" asked Lightning. "I thought that was one of the toughest challenges we've ever had to face."

"That wasn't so bad," Sarge said. "It was like standard basic training in the army."

"Those two weeks was the bestest of my life," Mater said. "I'd do it all over again if you asked me!"

"Seriously? You actually enjoyed all those grueling drills?" Lightning asked.

"Sure did! I got to spend time with my closest buddies," Mater replied.

"Yeah, man, it was like we became one mind," said Fillmore.

Lightning smiled. "I have to admit, it was an amazing experience. It was also exhausting. Why don't I tell you what those two weeks were like from my point of view."

"Let's hear it, then," Sarge said.

"Dadgum!" Mater exclaimed. "Is it time for another story? Hold on, I've gotta get comfy for this." He drove around the campfire twice, finally chose a nice, warm spot to settle into, and snagged a steaming cup of oil with his tow hook. "Okay, I'm ready—hit it, buddy!"

Chapter 10

"I was sound asleep one night at the Cozy Cone Motel, dreaming of the checkered flag, when I had a rude awakening.

And his name was Doc.

'C'mon kid, it's time.'

'Wha—? What time is it?' I stammered, blinking at the clock. 'What are you doing in my cone? Did Sally let—'

'You became a hero in that last Piston Cup race. Now it's time you became a winner,' said Doc.

'Oh, no,' I said, closing my eyes. 'We're not doing this now, are we?'

It had only been a few days since the Piston

Cup tiebreaker race, and Doc was already eager to begin training. He was really into his new role as my crew chief.

'Doc, I had that race won. I held myself back because I wanted to help The King. I think I still did pretty good.'

'Good? That's what you strive to be?' Doc asked. 'Good isn't going to cut it—not in the Piston Cup. Our two-week training course starts now.' He rolled out of my cone.

'Can't sleep be my first lesson?' I grumbled to myself.

Doc was waiting for me in the middle of Main Street. The moonlight was shining down on him.

'Here's what we're going to do,' he said. 'We're going to build the best racing team there ever was. You, me, Mack, Luigi, Guido, Mater, Sarge, and Fillmore. We need to learn how to work as a team. Be more than the sum of our parts.'

'I love the idea of getting the band back together,' I said. 'But I'm sure those guys are sleeping, too.'

'No, right now it's just you and me.'

And that's how it started. While you guys were sleeping the night away, Doc had me out there at Willys Butte under the stars. I was working on my turns, and passing, and accelerating through the straightaways. We did that until sunrise, and then all you guys showed up for pit-stop practice.

We set up a makeshift pit on the side of the dirt track. I remember thinking those drills were the worst! Doc made me put on a blindfold. Then Luigi and Guido gave me a new set of tires, Mater tossed away the old ones, and Fillmore gassed me up.

'That blindfold should help you listen to what's happening,' Doc said, his eyes on his stopwatch. 'Can you hear each of your crew members? Can you tell when they're almost finished? You guys need to act as a unit.'

After we completed the drill, I'd pull out of the pit and Doc would stop the clock.

'Too slow,' he said. 'Faster.'

Then he put the blindfolds on all of us. That

was a disaster. In fact, Guido put my tires on Fillmore by accident. Remember that?

Doc was not happy. 'You're not listening to each other!' he said.

Then he had me race you guys with that lousy blindfold on. He drove right next to me, always talking.

'Can you hear the other cars?' he asked. Where are they? Feel the vibrations they make on the track. Smell their tires.'

'Smell their tires?' I shouted with my blindfold on. 'That is not a thing!'

'The point is, you need to get out of your head,' Doc said when we stopped. 'See the big picture. Feel all the cars around you at once. You should anticipate the gaps between the cars before they actually happen, and be ready to make your move.'

'You want me to do all that going two hundred miles per hour?'

'Once you listen hard enough, all will become quiet,' he said. 'It'll seem like things are moving in slow motion. Then you'll be able to navigate through the other racers like they're standing still.'

After a week of that kind of training, I had to be honest with Doc. 'I don't think this is working,' I told him. 'Our times aren't any better.'

'Just be patient,' he said. 'It'll come.'

That's when Doc asked Sarge to help out with some strength conditioning. I pulled ol' Bessie, the road-paving machine, and pushed Mack around the track while he stayed in neutral. Then the whole team raced up the sand dunes. We lost Guido three times and had to dig him out.

While we were doing all this strength training, Doc was busy designing lighter equipment so we could move faster during our pit stops. He built a smaller jack for Luigi and a lightweight compressed-air wrench for Guido. He created a specialized fuel can that was easier for Fillmore to lift. He even built Mater a chain with a double hook so he could yank away two tires at once.

And the drills just kept coming. Remember we did a pit stop while balancing oil cans on our roofs? Where did Doc come up with that stuff?

With one day left in our two-week training camp, we executed a perfect pit stop, which beat Doc's goal for us by two full seconds. I couldn't believe it!

I thanked Doc for everything he'd taught me and the whole pit crew—and for all his patience and confidence in us. 'There was a time I thought I'd always be a one-man show,' I told him. 'But now I actually like being part of a team. Helping each other. Pushing ourselves. Digging Guido out together.'

'You did good, kid,' said Doc. 'I'm proud of all of you. You're ready.'

I never told you guys back then, but you all inspired me. After those two weeks, I no longer wanted to win my first Piston Cup. I wanted *us* to win *our* first Piston Cup."

Chapter 11

Early the next morning, the campsite was still soggy, but at least the rain had not returned.

Lightning woke up to the sound of sniffling. He rolled out of his tent to find Mater staring into the tiny bit of glow left in the campfire.

"Mater, why are you up so early?" he asked.

Mater jolted in surprise; he hadn't heard Lightning approach. "Aw, shucks, sorry," he said, sniffling. "I didn't mean to wake you."

"It's okay. I just thought I heard—" Lightning paused. "Are you all right, Mater?"

"Oh, I guess I'm just a bit sad," Mater said, blinking.

"Why? What's up, buddy?" Lightning asked,

rolling closer. "Aren't you enjoying our camping trip?"

"I'm loving it! I'm just sad we're leaving today," he said. "I wish we could stay. I can't remember ever havin' so much fun. Makes me realize how the time we all get to spend together is so important."

"Aw, Mater, you're fogging me up," Lightning said.

"You know what," Mater said, "I'll just grab this tree and refuse to let go. Then we can't leave, unless we take this tree with us."

"Why don't we leave the trees here," Lightning said, smiling. "You're right about one thing, though. This camping trip has been amazing. The pinecones, the storm, the caves . . ."

"Your stories, that ravine," Mater said. "And Fillmore's snoring."

"Not sure which was scarier—the ravine or the snoring," Lightning said, chuckling. "Probably the snoring. The first night, I thought Frank the combine had tracked us down." Lightning laughed quietly. "Hey, you know what? We'll go camping again, for sure. This has been great. And we don't even have to wait till next year."

"Really?" Mater exclaimed. "How about tomorrow?"

Before Lightning could reply, Fillmore emerged from his tent. "Whoa, it's so early, it's still late," he said.

"Sorry for waking you," Lightning said. "We're just sad to see this little expedition come to an end."

"Oh, that's right," Fillmore said, shaking off the sleep. "I've got a special organic fuel mix I've been saving for the drive back home."

"That organic stuff always gives me the backfires," Mater mumbled to Lightning.

"Is that what I was hearing the other night?" Lightning said, nudging his best buddy.

Sarge exited his tent, ready to wake his

campmates with the bugle call, when he spotted the other three staring at him.

"Oh," he said in surprise. He cleared his throat. "I ... uh ... I must have overslept."

"The world is upside down if I'm up before him," Fillmore said.

"I'll get the fire going," Sarge said, yawning.

"Never seen him yawn before, either," Fillmore whispered. "I'm kind of freaking out over here."

While Sarge started the fire, Lightning told him they had been discussing how much he and Mater had enjoyed the camping trip.

"Classic bonding," Sarge said. "Happens in the military. The shared experience is a powerful thing."

Lightning sighed. "It's like when we truly became a team and won our first Piston Cup. That was one of the best moments of my life."

"I was good, wasn't I?" Mater said. "If you don't say so yourself."

"I think you just did," Lightning said with a chuckle.

"Just goes to show you the value of basic

training and repeated drills," Sarge said.

Lightning closed his eyes and smiled. "I can remember every second of that first win like it was yesterday."

"We've got time for one more story," Fillmore said.

"I could tell that story from now until the tractors come home," Lightning said.

"We don't have that much time," Sarge said.

"Okay, okay," Lightning said. "It all started with Doc being a no-show."

"A no-show?" Sarge said. "That's not how I remember it."

"Well, then I better get started," Lightning said. "You guys are going to love this."

Chapter 12

"My arrival at the Los Angeles International Speedway was totally different from my previous appearance. The first time, it was all about the photos and the reporters and the sponsors and the TV cameras. This time, my pit crew isolated me from the crowd while the hubbub went on around me.

I remember staying close to Sarge, who kept yelling, 'No interviews! Make way! Let him through!' He was great. It was like I had my own private motorcade!

Once we were in the pits, we went through the prerace routine that Doc had gone over with us. Since we had gotten there early enough, I

had the chance to take a few laps to get a feel for the track. Then we had a pit-crew meeting to check all the equipment and make sure we were all in sync.

I did well at the time-qualifier, but I was careful not to show off. I was saving myself for the main event.

After the qualifier, I headed straight back to

the pits to be with my crew and focus on the race. Everything was going as planned. There was just one thing missing: Doc. I hadn't seen him at all since we'd arrived. I figured he was checking the track conditions or talking with the race officials, but he hadn't been in touch with anyone on the crew. That wasn't like him.

'Hey, where's Doc?' I asked Luigi.

'I keep track of tires,' Luigi told me. 'Nobody told Luigi to keep track of Doc, too.'

'All right, Number 95, time to move into position,' a race official told me.

I looked around, but Doc was nowhere to be found.

A few minutes before the green flag dropped, my headset came to life.

'Good morning, Team 95.'

'Doc? Is that you? Where have you been?' I asked.

'I've been watching from a distance,' Doc replied. 'I'm trying to give you some space. Last thing you need is an ol' grandpa car making you nervous.'

"I'm glad you're here, Doc," I said. "I couldn't do this without you."

The green flag dropped, and the race got under way. I fell into a comfortable middle-of-the-pack position, just as we had planned. The first forty laps flew by, and I was getting anxious. I saw the other cars looking at me funny. *They think I've lost my mojo*, I realized.

'Doc, I'm in the thick of it here. Everyone is going to think something's wrong with me.'

'Don't let them get to you,' Doc said. 'Remember, this time we're racing *our* race, not the race everyone else is expecting. We can start flexing at lap eighty.'

'Patience is hard work,' I said.

The first pit stop was a blur. All that practice paid off as we let our instincts take over.

'Have a nice day,' Mater said before I pulled back out onto the track, just as we had practiced a million times. I couldn't help smiling.

'Now, *that* was a pit stop,' Doc said.

Finally, I reached lap eighty. I was still in the middle of the pack, but I was feeling okay with it.

'All right, kid,' Doc said, 'we're exactly where we want to be. Remember, we plan our work and we work our plan. Time for Lightning to strike.'

'I'm ready, Doc,' I said.

I felt like I had so much left in the tank. I started to pick my spots, and I moved through the field of racers one by one.

'Don't force it.' Doc reminded me. 'Lap by lap, keep climbing through them. Feel the openings before they happen. Let them come to you.'

Moments later, I felt like a switch had been flipped and all the bright lights and noises faded away. It was just me and the racetrack. And as strange as this sounds, everything seemed to slow down. I was going over two hundred miles an hour, but I swear I was moving in slow motion.

'You're doing good, kid. There's another gap—yep, you got it.' Doc kept talking to me through the headset. 'Keep squeezing through!'

With thirty-five laps to go, we executed our last pit stop. Everything went smoothly.

'You're in the zone now,' Fillmore said before I shot away.

'Just so you know, that was our best time ever for a pit stop,' Doc said.

With the wind against my face and my wheels skimming the asphalt like water, I felt like I was flying. I tapped my reserves in those final laps. I poured on the speed as my eyes locked on to the checkered flag. The entire stadium erupted with cheers when I crossed the finish line. I had won by three car lengths! I heard Mater whooping and hollering. And on my headset, I heard Doc's calm, gravelly voice: 'You've got a lotta stuff, kid.'

I did a few celebratory doughnuts on the track as the crowd chanted, "Lightning! Lightning! Lightning!" Then I made my way over to Victory Lane to accept the Piston Cup trophy. It was like a dream. That moment was the culmination of my whole racing career. I had never been so proud of a win before.

But, as thrilling as Victory Lane was—with all the cheers, confetti, and interviews—the moment that was even more meaningful to me was a much quieter one. After the excitement had died down, a photographer asked if he could take a picture of just me and Doc.

I remember that Doc looked so proud up there on the crew-chief stand as we posed for a photo together with the Piston Cup trophy. Sharing the win with him and our whole team was the best feeling in the world."

Chapter 13

"**A**re those pinecones?" Sarge asked.

The foursome had packed up their campsite, hit the road, and were now stopped next to a big grassy meadow.

"Those sure do look like pinecones to me," Lightning said, smiling.

Sarge grinned. "Last one out there is a burned-out spark plug!" He shot into the meadow and began crunching pinecones with his tires.

"Is that our Sarge?" Fillmore asked. "I never knew he could be so . . . spontaneous."

"Apparently crushing pinecones is now considered mission-critical," Lightning said.

The others looked at each other for a moment, then raced out to join the fun. Soon they had crunched every last pinecone.

"Why did I wait so long to enjoy that unique experience?" Sarge said.

"Maybe we should put you in charge of fun and games next time," Lightning said.

Sarge cleared his throat and looked at the others. "Before we get back," he began, "I just wanted to tell you that it's been an honor working—and camping—with you all. It makes me proud to have served as your teammate." He looked away, blinking.

"Don't mind them tears, Sarge. Crushing pinecones stirs up all kinds of emotions," Mater said.

"MOVE OUT!" Sarge boomed suddenly, and he pulled back onto the road, leading the way. The others fell into formation behind him as they began the last leg of their journey.

When the campers arrived home, all their friends came out to greet them on Main Street.

"You survived!" Sally said.

"Not only did we survive, we thrived!" Lightning exclaimed. "I had a great time, Sal."

"I'm glad, Stickers," replied Sally. "And it's good to have you home."

"Hey, everyone," Lightning called. "I just want to let you all know that Mater was named our MVC—Most Valuable Camper."

"I was?" Mater shouted. "Holy tire! I've never won anything in my life! I'd like to thank my buddies, the creek that put out my fire, and all the pinecones I had to roll over to get here."

Just then, Mack arrived to announce that he had Harv on the phone.

"Lightning, are you there?" Harv's voice squawked through the speaker.

"Hey, Harv! I'm back and no worse for wear," Lightning answered.

"Good," Harv said, "because the race is back on in four days."

"YES!" Lightning exclaimed. "That's great news, Harv! And you know what? I really feel like my batteries are recharged."

Luigi rushed over. "Ah! *Fantástico!* Guido, bring the tires and—" He paused, giving Lightning's muddy tires a disapproving look. "Pack a set of Glidewells. Lightning needs a tire change already."

"I'm ready to hit the road whenever you are, boss," Mack said.

Mater slowly rolled up to Lightning. "I guess yer probably rarin' to go," he said. "I'm really gonna miss you, buddy."

Lightning looked at Mater, Sarge, and Fillmore.

"You know, I think I'm going to need my full pit crew at this race. What do you say, guys? Are you up for more bonding time?"

"WA-HOOOOO!" Mater hollered, jumping a few feet off the ground. "More bonding time! And I didn't even have to tie myself to a tree!"

Fillmore smiled. "Totally, man. Count me in!"

Sarge stepped up. "Reporting for duty!"

"Then there's just one thing left to do before we go," Lightning said. "Flo, break out your best oil. The first round's on me, everyone!"

"You got it, darlin'. Let's toast to Team McQueen!" Flo said.

Everyone cheered and headed to the V8 Café.

Mater drove up alongside Lightning. "Hey, buddy," he said, "if you liked this camping trip, just think what the next one'll be like. We'll have even more stories to tell!"

"You're right, Mater," Lightning said. "We have a lot to look forward to."

"Starting now," Mater said. "Race ya to the V8!"

Lightning flashed a smile. *"Ka-chow!"*

The End

"So where'd he come from?"

I can't tell you how often I get that question. Everyone is curious and a little bit baffled. And I'm here to set the record straight.

I'm Ray Reverham, the hard-driving crew chief for racing's surprise sensation, Jackson Storm. He's the out-of-nowhere superstar everybody has been talking about since his big win at Copper Canyon Speedway.

I come from a family of crew chiefs. I guess you could say racing is the family business. I've seen a lot of crazy things in my years running racing teams, but I've never experienced anything quite like the Jackson Storm story.

The crazy rumors I hear about Storm always give me a good laugh. I've been asked if Jackson Storm was made in a laboratory from spare parts by a mad scientist. I've also heard the theory that he's controlled remotely by a supercomputer with artificial intelligence. There's even a rumor that his engine came from an alien spaceship that crash-landed in the desert.

Let me start with the fact that, while they're exciting, these theories are nonsense. Jackson Storm is simply a very fast, very talented race car with an unlikely background.

So what's his deal, then? Where did he come from? How does someone just cruise onto the racing scene like that, without anyone seeing him coming? It's really no mystery. It's just that he didn't take the usual path to Piston Cup stardom.

It all started when I received an invitation from Axle P. Biggs, a business tycoon. I had no idea what I was in for when I arrived at his headquarters high atop the Biggs Tower.

"Welcome, Ray!" Biggs boomed. "May I call you Chief?"

"Sure, everybody does," I replied, following him into his spacious office.

"I'm a man of action, not words, Chief, so let me cut right to the chase: I'm preparing to shock the racing world. And I want to know if you're interested in coming along for the ride."

"Okay," I said, distracted by the panoramic views of Los Angeles from his office windows.

"Beautiful, isn't it?" Biggs said. "When you're this high up, the sky's the limit. That's exactly what I was thinking when I made plans to build the most advanced racing facility in the world."

"I didn't know Biggs Industries was involved with racing," I said.

"Well, I wasn't, until my son A. P. Biggs Jr. showed interest in the sport," Biggs replied. "He gave me the idea to win a Piston Cup."

I smiled. "You can't just build a pricey facility and expect to win a Piston Cup," I told him.

"Well, you haven't seen this racing facility yet," Biggs said. He rolled over to a table, where I saw a model of the proposed racing facility. I could tell he was proud of it. "The Biggs Industries Racing

Complex will feature the most technologically advanced training equipment. And you, Chief, will help me find and train racing's next superstar."

"The process is a little more complicated than that," I replied.

"Listen, Chief," he said, rolling behind his massive desk. "I'm an entrepreneur. I started my business empire with computer software, then an Internet search engine, and most recently, security systems—all areas I had no experience in. I know how to identify opportunities and hire the experts and talent to help me achieve my objectives. So why should racing be any different?"

"There are just a lot of factors involved in winning a Piston Cup," I told him.

"You leave those factors up to me," he said. "Your job is to focus on finding the 'next big thing' for Team Biggs. I know you're looking for a new opportunity. I know you were the crew chief for a legendary Piston Cup champion. You know what's required to get to the top. I think you should come aboard and give this a shot."

It was true. I was looking for an opportunity, as my last racer had recently retired. I was between race cars, as they say. However, I was nervous about working for someone outside the racing business. But Biggs was right: I needed the job, and the challenge was certainly unique. "It sounds interesting," I said.

"That's what I thought you'd say!" Biggs exclaimed. "Now go find me my champion."

I couldn't help laughing out loud. "That's much easier said than done. Searching for the next big racing star isn't like—"

"Chief, I have no doubt that you're up to the task," Biggs said, cutting me off. "Just remember, we have to move quickly. They don't call me Speedy Biggs for nothing!"

So I headed out to the heart of Piston Cup country to recruit ten racers. I called every connection I had. I traveled far and wide, attended more than a hundred junior-league races, and visited as many racing academies. I chased down rumors about street racers. I chatted up reporters for tips about up-and-coming speedsters. I scouted every place I could think of for rookie talent that I could mold.

I managed to round up nine young racers in the nick of time. The Biggs Industries Racing Complex opened three weeks ahead of schedule—and it really was the most technically advanced training facility I had ever seen.

The racers immediately began training on the simulators and treadmills. While they showed a lot of promise, they were an inexperienced lot. They were also spoiled, and it was difficult to push them to their limits. There was only one racer, Tim Treadless, who seemed fast enough to qualify for a Piston Cup race, but I knew it would take a lot of work. Not one of them was the instant, out-of-the-box star Biggs wanted.

"I expected more from you, Chief," he said. "I gave you the facility, and you rounded up the best you could find, but there's nobody here who has star potential. My data expert is reviewing each racer's data on the simulator, and he is concerned."

He had good reason for concern. But so far,

all we had was racing simulator data, which didn't give us a complete picture of the racers' capabilities and talent. We still needed to see the racers on a real track. In my opinion, there wasn't any kind of high-tech training that could take the place of real dirt and asphalt.

I sighed. "Give me a little more time with them," I said.

"I don't want to drag this out," said Biggs. "We have room for one more racer on this team. Find me a winner by the end of the week, or I'll need to find someone who can."

I don't want to say I was desperate, but I needed a miracle. And you won't believe where I found it.

**Continue to read about the
rise of Jackson Storm in the next
Cars Origins adventure!**